For Mum and Dad

Text copyright © Jonny Zucker, 2008
Illustrations copyright © Ned Woodman, 2008

"Mission 3: In Deep" was originally published in English in 2008. This edition is published by an arrangement with STRIPES PUBLISHING, an imprint of Magi Publications.

Copyright © 2013 by Darby Creek

Darby Creek
A division of Lerner Publishing Group, Inc.
241 First Avenue North
Minneapolis, MN 55401 U.S.A.

Website address: www.lernerbooks.com

Library of Congress Cataloging-in-Publication Data

Zucker, Jonny.
In deep / by Jonny Zucker ; illustrated by Ned Woodman.
    pages   cm. — (Max Flash ; mission 3)
Originally published in the United Kingdom by Stripes Publishing, 2008.
Summary: "Max is told that an island in the Indian Ocean has been flooded by a freak surge of water. The DFEA suspects sinister underwater forces are at work, and Max can't wait to dive into his third mission."— Provided by publisher.
    ISBN 978-1-4677-1209-5 (lib. bdg. : alk. paper)
    ISBN 978-1-4677-2053-3 (eBook)
[1. Underwater exploration—Fiction. 2. Adventure and adventurers—Fiction.]
I. Woodman, Ned, 1978– illustrator. II. Title.
PZ7.Z77925In 2013
[Fic]—dc23   2012049021

Manufactured in the United States of America
1 – BP – 7/15/13

MISSION3
IN DEEP

Jonny Zucker

Illustrated by
Ned Woodman

CHAPTER 1

Max Flash vaulted over a high concrete wall.
He thudded down on the other side. He could
hear the crunch of Alton's footsteps close
behind. He sprinted down a twisting track.
He spotted a rope up ahead, hanging from
a wooden beam. Max grabbed it and started
climbing upward. Seconds later he swung onto
the beam and glanced back. Alton was gaining
on him.

Max darted across the top, willing himself
to keep his balance on the narrow surface. He

reached the end and looked down. The drop was pretty steep. But there was no turning back. He launched himself through the air and crashed down onto a bed of leaves. He bent his knees to cushion his fall.

I've got to move faster!

Max sped off up the path. Alton's feet hit the turf and came straight after him. Max quickened his pace. Up ahead were two giant oak trees with a very narrow gap between them.

I have to make it through first!

Max thundered on. He suddenly felt a vicious stab of pain in the heel of his left foot. Alton had kicked out and struck him. Max gritted his teeth. The gap in the trees was approaching fast. Suddenly he heard a whoosh of air as Alton sprung forward, aiming a kung fu kick at Max's head. In a split second, Max darted to his left. He dove toward the gap. As he sailed through, he

heard a cry as Alton's body smashed against one of the trees.

Max skidded on his front over the ground and came to a stop. Slowly he got to his feet and looked around. Alton was climbing through the gap in the trees, panting, limping, and looking completely humiliated.

"Good work, Max," Alton puffed. "I've been a DFEA agent for ten years. Plus, I designed this assault course. And you STILL beat me. You've upped your game."

CHAPTER 2

Max was about to reply when a robotic voice boomed, "Max Flash, report to Room 17 immediately." A green arrow flashed on the wall.

"Better not keep Zavonne waiting," said Max.

Alton nodded. "Not a good idea! But watch out, Max. I'll get you next time."

Max followed the arrow to the end of the wall and rounded the corner. In front of him was a low, gray building. A black shutter lifted quickly. Max stepped inside.

He found himself in a long, windowless corridor with a row of numbered doors on the left side. Max was just about to knock on the one marked Room 17 when it silently swung open. Inside was a rectangular, sterile room with a metal table and two chairs.

Zavonne was seated at the table. Her hair was pulled tightly back off her face. Her cold, clear eyes followed Max as he walked over and sat down facing her.

He had met Zavonne before, but only as a figure on the computer screen. It was weird to see she was a human after all.

Zavonne worked for an organization called the DFEA—the Department for Extraordinary Activity. They dealt with "unusual" cases that were too weird for the normal forces of law and order. Max's parents were stage magicians by day. They had carried out two missions for the Department several years ago. Max had been recruited by Zavonne a while back. He'd already completed two death-defying missions. One was in the Virtual world and another in the furthest reaches of outer space. Max had incredible contortionist and escapology skills honed through years of taking part in his parents' stage show. These abilities made him the perfect candidate for both of those missions.

Zavonne had instructed Max to spend all day at the secret DFEA training center, testing

his physical strength to the limit. His race with Alton on the assault course had been his toughest challenge and a close contest.

"Alton is one of our fittest operatives," said Zavonne coolly. "And yet you made it to the end without getting caught."

Max nodded. He allowed himself a small smile. He guessed he was being trained for his third mission. But what would it be?

"Something's come up," said Zavonne swiftly. "Way out in the Pacific Ocean is a very remote island called Decca. It served as a Ministry of Defense base for half a century. Two years ago, the Ministry made a strategic decision to close it down. All that remains on the island is an old army barracks and a memorial statue. There's also a lighthouse to warn ships about the treacherous rocks surrounding the island. The Ministry is still responsible for the upkeep of the lighthouse. They visit the island twice a year."

s eyes were locked on Zavonne's as he
every word.

"Last week," Zavonne continued, "two Ministry technicians visited Decca Island for one of these lighthouse checks. A violent storm struck as they were preparing to leave. Ferocious waves smashed onto the island and completely flooded it. The two technicians nearly drowned as they attempted to take refuge in the lighthouse."

Max looked at Zavonne blankly. *So?*

"The Ministry concluded it was a freak storm. But the DFEA doesn't share that analysis."

"Why is the DFEA interested in some island in the middle of nowhere?" asked Max.

"The area around Decca Island is rich in sailors' tales about mermaids and sea monsters," Zavonne said. "We at the DFEA know many of these stories are just legends. Still, we've always kept an eye on the island and the waters surrounding it."

Max blinked in surprise. *Is Zavonne sending me on a mermaid hunt?*

"So we sent a specialist marine team to investigate."

"What did they discover?" asked Max.

"Absolutely nothing," replied Zavonne. "So we instructed them to dive and investigate below the waterline."

"Did they find anything?"

Zavonne's gaze hardened. "They were less than a mile down when they were attacked."

"Attacked? By who?"

"By sharks," Zavonne said. "At least, that's what they initially thought. It all happened so fast, and they were obviously focused on getting out of the water as fast as possible. The creatures coming at our men looked like sharks. But they didn't move like sharks. This was a dangerous situation. Understandably, the crew did not investigate further."

"Were they hurt?"

"No one was seriously injured apart from a few cuts and bruises. But this attack on our divers and the storm on the island have set off alarm bells. Both incidents were hostile toward humans. This has led us to suspect some kind of USCs are living down there."

"USCs?" asked Max.

"Unidentified Sea Creatures," explained Zavonne. "We believe that these attacks are linked. We don't know who these creatures are or where they come from. We don't know what they're planning. We don't know how powerful they are. We need to find answers to these questions as quickly as possible. Any delay could spell disaster."

So what's my role going to be in all of this?

"The DFEA has spent the last few years developing a new material called Stealth Film," said Zavonne.

"What's that got to do with sea creatures

and the island?" asked Max.

"When Stealth Film covers the human body, the wearer can breathe normally underwater without an oxygen tank," replied Zavonne. A diver covered in Stealth Film can dive much deeper than anyone using even the most up-to-date diving gear. You can swim when you're wearing this Film. It also has a special technology. This lets the wearer walk on solid surfaces underwater, like rock formations and the seabed."

Cool!

"We have created the world's first Second Skin Suit using Stealth Film. It covers one's clothing and cannot be detected at all."

A concealed metal drawer at the side of the table suddenly opened. Inside was a garment made of super thin, see-through material.

Max stared at it. "Wow! You've made all of those DFEA divers Second Skin Suits so they can go back down and investigate these scary USCs?"

"Stealth Film is an incredibly complex material to make," Zavonne continued. "It's also very, very expensive. As a result, we only had enough material for one Suit. Pick it up."

Max leaned over and pulled the Suit toward him. It unfurled and rested against his body. It was his exact size. He looked from the Suit to Zavonne and back again.

"You . . . you want me to go down there?" he asked.

"One Suit. Your size," said Zavonne pointedly.

"Why don't you just wait a bit longer? You

could make some more Stealth Film and build some bigger Suits?" asked Max.

Zavonne shook her head. "First, there is no time. Second, there is another aspect of the Suit that fits your profile. We have conducted a battery of underwater tests on the Suit. But it is still only a prototype. The Suit has never been used in real mission conditions. We cannot be a hundred percent certain of its reliability."

Oh great!

"I've studied the water-based escape acts you perform in your parents' show, Max. You have a strong ability to hold your breath under water for long periods. You will be able to get up to the surface more safely than any other DFEA operative if the Second Skin Suit does malfunction."

A deep sea mission is a bit more dangerous than escaping from a water tank in Mom and Dad's stage show.

Max eyed Zavonne. "I can hold my breath for three minutes," he mused. "But what happens if the Suit breaks and it's more than a three-minute journey to the surface?"

"I am assuming that scenario won't happen," Zavonne replied. "And after today, I'm satisfied with your fitness and stamina levels . . . But make no mistake, this could be a very dangerous mission."

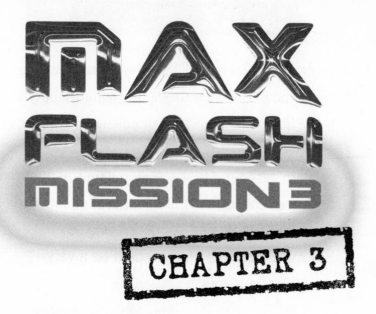

MISSION3

CHAPTER 3

Max looked expectantly at Zavonne. "Er, any chance of some gadgets?" he asked.

"I haven't forgotten," Zavonne replied. She reached down and picked up a black metallic case from the floor. She laid it on the table and flicked open the catches. Reaching inside, she picked up a green-and-black marble with a tiny red button on its surface and handed it to Max.

"There are specially concealed pockets in the Suit for your gadgets," she explained.

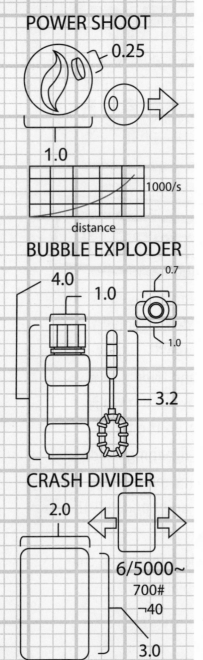

POWER SHOOT

0.25

1.0

1000/s

distance

BUBBLE EXPLODER

4.0

1.0

0.7

1.0

3.2

CRASH DIVIDER

2.0

6/5000~
700#
¬40

3.0

"This is a Power Shoot. Pressing the red button will cause a giant explosion of compressed air to shoot from the holder a hundred meters upward. It works underwater or on land."

Excellent!

Max took the marble and placed it in a pocket of the Second Skin Suit. Zavonne then held up a small bottle of bubbles like the ones he'd had as a kid. She unscrewed the lid and pulled out the bubble ring. "This is a Bubble Exploder. Blow into this bubble ring, and millions of bubbles are instantly

released. They will momentarily blind and disorient anyone within a thirty-meter radius."

She replaced the ring in the bottle and passed it over.

"And this is a Crash Divider," said Zavonne. She held up what looked like a standard football trading card.

Max turned it over in his hands.

"Slip this between a door and its frame or between any sort of sliding panels. It will force a narrow opening for exactly five seconds, allowing you time to get through."

Max tucked it away safely and eyed Zavonne. "So when am I going?" he asked.

"You leave tonight."

Max gulped. *Thanks for the warning!*

"Oh, and one last thing," noted Zavonne.

She does have feelings after all! She's going to wish me good luck.

"Bring back the Second Skin Suit in one piece," she said curtly.

MAX FLASH MISSION 3

CHAPTER 4

Snub flicked a switch The boat glided to a halt.

Snub was a tall man with a large chin, narrow eyes, and a thick covering of stubble. He cut an imposing figure. He also was the DFEA operative charged with getting Max to the start of his mission. Max had hoped Snub might offer him some advice, but he was clearly a man of few words. They'd been on the boat for two hours, following a very speedy flight on a DFEA jet. Snub had barely said anything at all.

Max touched the collar of the Second Skin

Suit that he wore over his wetsuit. He still couldn't believe that this flimsy film was going to work. It covered his entire body, yet he couldn't feel it at all. It was just like having a second skin.

"OK," said Snub. "We'll reach your dive entry point very soon. This is the place where our divers were attacked. They reported that the sharks came at them from directly below. So you need to head straight down. I want you in the water quickly so I can get the boat away without attracting attention. I will remain just outside the mission zone as directed. Pull that blue cord on your suit when you need me. I'll be with you in about ten minutes. Any questions?"

Max shivered nervously and shook his head. Snub gave him an encouraging nod and started the engine. Five minutes later, he cut the motor again. He gave Max the thumbs-up.

This is it! No going back!

Max pulled the hood of the Second Skin Suit over his head and closed the seal. He stepped over to the edge and peered down into the watery depths. He felt a sudden stab of fear.

It's great that I've got a nice, easy mission for my first ever underwater adventure!

He took a deep breath and dived.

MISSION 3

CHAPTER 5

It took Max several minutes to get used to
the sensation of swimming with the Second
Skin Suit on. He was surrounded by water,
but it felt like he wasn't in the sea. He could
breathe normally. The water made no impact
on his body. But the amazing sights he passed
reminded him exactly where he was. Here was
a huge row of glowing orange anemones. There
was a gigantic silver-and-pink fish. The sights
were magnificent, but he remembered what
had happened to the DFEA divers. *What if a*

*group of those weird sharks is hiding behind
that rock? What if some piranhas pounce and
make me their afternoon snack?*

The water changed as he dived deeper. At
times it was crystal clear. And then it would
turn muddy and restrict his vision. Deeper
and deeper he went. He passed a huge school
of long, bright-blue fish. He almost collided
with a line of swordfish. One swam right up
to his face for closer inspection. He swam
right through a colossal formation of yellow
and black rocks and traveled beside a group
of turquoise stingrays. Max gave a wide berth
to a tight pack of spiky green fish with sharp-
looking teeth.

He had been swimming for about half an
hour without any sign of murky goings-on
when Max started to feel frustrated. Could
Zavonne have been mistaken? Maybe he
wouldn't find anything, no matter long and
deep he dived.

A few minutes later, he spotted something in the distance. It looked like a pale and distant light.

Perhaps it's an electric eel . . . or a whole bunch of them!

Intrigued, Max swam on. The light became a bit brighter and a whole lot bigger with each stroke. He opened his mouth in complete amazement as he swam toward it.

It wasn't one light. It was a series of lights. He saw a high fence that stretched for miles.

Max stared in disbelief. It was some kind of underwater city on the seafloor. Max was sure of it. He could see buildings and carefully planted sea plants that looked like trees. But was anyone inside the settlement? Were they the ones who attacked the other divers? Or was it completely deserted and not connected to the USCs in any way?

Max swam slowly towards the settlement and tried to take it all in. It was huge.

Time to check out my ability to walk in water wearing the Second Skin Suit!

Max straightened up and lowered his feet to the ground. He touched down and stayed put. He took a couple of steps. And then a few more. It was incredible! He was walking on the bottom of the seafloor. And it felt like he was walking down his local main street. The water didn't hold him back at all.

He broke into a run. *I'm going to be the world's first underwater 100-meter sprinter!*

Max forced himself to focus on his mission. He skidded to a stop. He looked up at the fence that stretched into the distance. He could easily swim over the top. But there were lots of powerful spotlights shining upward. What if someone saw him? It would be best to stay hidden until he could find out where he was.

Max walked along the fence. He studied it for the slightest weakness. He found it a few minutes later. A small section of the fence's metal twine had come undone.

Perfect!

Max began to carefully enlarge the hole. He unthreaded the twine until he had opened up a small gap.

He pushed his hand through to widen the hole.

The second he did, a harsh beeping sounded out. *An alarm! There must be a trip wire behind the fence!*

Max stared at the fence. The gap was nowhere near the size he wanted it.

What if I rip my Suit getting through?

An automated voice said, "INTRUDER ALERT! INTRUDER ALERT!"

There was no time to lose. Max contorted his body expertly and just managed to squeeze through.

The alarm screeched on. So did the robot warning, "INTRUDER ALERT!"

Stay around and wait for the welcoming party? I don't think so!

"INTRUDER ALERT!" shrieked the voice.

Max dropped to the seafloor on the other side of the hole and ran. Ahead of him was a series of tall, gray buildings. He ran past these.

He turned left into a deserted alleyway. It was flanked by high, brown walls. At the end of the alley was an archway carved into a block of stone. Max leaned against the stone and caught his breath.

CHAPTER 6

The powerful alarm voice stopped as suddenly as it had begun. Max waited to see if it would be activated again. It wasn't. He waited another few seconds. Then he peered through the archway. A very busy thoroughfare stretched to the left and right. A huge street sign on a high building read, MAIN STREET—AQUATROPOLIS.

Aquatropolis!

This wasn't some tiny backwater town. This was an entire city! And it was populated by the

zzling array of bizarre-looking creatures.
were half-human, half-fish. Max could hardly
elieve his eyes. Some had lobster heads and
human lower halves. Others had grungy human
teenager tops and swordfish bottom halves.
There was even a couple with goldfish heads on
top of chunky human legs dressed in lederhosen.

Unreal!

Max saw that some male and female
creatures with human top halves wore colorful
wraps around their bottom fish-halves.

*I need one of those wraps. I can't step out
with a whole human body. I'll stick out like a
whole human sore thumb.*

He watched the creatures going about their
day. Some of them were swimming. Others
were walking. Several were just floating along.
They were busy chatting, riding bikes, and
behaving like humans.

*How weird is this?! It's just like a human
city, but underwater. Who are these people?*

Max quickly scanned the buildings on the street. There was a bar called The Algae & Anemone. A group of creatures with salmon heads and bulky human bottom halves drank from huge pint glasses and sang raucous songs. Farther down was a shiny steel building called the H2O Center. Outside the building there was a faded poster for a concert by CURT AND THE WHALERS. Next to that was a fancy-looking restaurant called Le Fin.

Max looked up and spotted a giant billboard. It was all white with a pair of beady brown eyes staring out above huge black letters: ARE YOU READY FOR RAY DAY?

Ray Day? Who is Ray? And what's his day about?

Max looked around. He checked Main Street and the alley he'd come from. About twenty meters down was a low wall. Behind it was a block of apartments. There were several washing lines hanging out next to the wall. Max guessed they had washing lines underwater to keep clothes straight. Drying them wasn't an option. Max was delighted to see a line holding some wraps.

He hurried over and unpegged a blue wrap. He tied it around his lower half. Max made sure it completely covered his legs and feet. He checked it and checked it again.

Perfect! I'll look just like one of them. I'm just glad my friends can't see me in a skirt!

Max hurried back down the alley and stepped out into the street. He tried not to stare at some of the creatures. But it was hard when they all looked so incredibly weird. He'd come across a secret underwater race! He passed a kids' playground. There were two tiny toddlers with the heads of eels whizzing down a slide.

On the other side of the playground was another poster. This one was the same ARE YOU READY FOR RAY DAY? sign. Max tried to make sense of it. This Ray guy with the beady eyes was obviously very central to whatever was going on down here.

Where can I get some decent info? I can't exactly introduce myself to someone and say, "Hi, I'm new around here. What evil plan are you guys hatching?"

Then something caught his eye. A long line of children was coming down the street. At the front was a boy. He had a sea bream head and a pudgy human lower half in baggy jeans and sneakers. At the back was a girl with an angelic human face. She had bright blue eyes and curly blonde hair—and octopus legs.

A scary-looking teacher with the head of a tuna was holding a clipboard. She tried to keep

control of the whole group. Max watched them pass and began to follow.

The teacher eventually stopped in front of a green building.

"Right, then," she said in a shrill voice. "I told you earlier, I'm standing in for Miss Rowntree today. I don't know all of your names. But you know my name. I'm Mrs. Flint. I want all of you to remember what we talked about back in class. A library is a place of silent learning. That means we all need to put our talking lips—human and fish—away."

Max spotted a sign on the side of the building: Aquatropolis Central Library.

Libraries and teachers . . . this is just like being at home! But at least I might find out some information about this place!

"Right 6B," trilled Mrs. Flint, "let's go inside in single file."

Max hurried over to join the back of the line. He watched as the children at the front of the

line shuffled in past the teacher. Mrs. Flint
checked off each one on her clipboard. The line
moved forward. Then the girl with the octopus
legs in front of Max turned around.

"Who are you?" she demanded.

"Who are you?" Max shot back.

"I'm Harriet. I'm in class 6B. And you?"

"Er . . . I'm just here for the day," Max
replied.

"For one day?" she asked suspiciously.

"It's Mrs. Flint," replied Max. "She's . . . er . . . she's . . . my mom."

The girl looked from Max to Mrs. Flint and back.

"Really?"

"Really." Max nodded.

"Oh. It's very uncool for your mom to be a teacher. I wouldn't mention it to the others." And with that she turned her back on him.

The line edged forward. There were now only seven kids between Max and Mrs. Flint. He quickly tapped Harriet on the shoulder. "Don't say anything to Mrs. Fl— I mean, my mom. She doesn't want anyone to know."

"I won't say anything," promised Harriet.

"Right," the teacher murmured to herself. Mrs. Flint checked off more children on her list. "Number thirty," she declared as Harriet reached her. "And that's the end of the . . ."

Suddenly Mrs. Flint looked up. She stared at Max. "What's going on?" she enquired. "I've already counted thirty pupils. That's the whole class. But you seem to be number thirty-one."

Max gulped.

Harriet nudged Mrs. Flint with her elbow and winked at the teacher. "Don't worry," she whispered. "You don't need to pretend you don't know him. Your secret's safe with me."

CHAPTER 7

Max cringed. His cover was about to be blown!

Mrs. Flint gave Harriet a funny stare. "What on earth are you talking about?" she asked.

"The extra kid. I know why he's here. He's your so—"

"I just LOVE libraries!" cried Max. He stepped on one of Harriet's octopus tentacles.

"Oww!" yelped Harriet.

"Yes!" Max continued. "Books are great. I love big books. Small books. Thin books. Fat books. Any kind of books."

Mrs. Flint looked completely bewildered.

"He just stepped on me," whined Harriet. She frantically hopped about on her other seven tentacles.

At that moment, there was a loud thud from inside the library. The boy at the front of the line had knocked over a large display of books. Mrs. Flint groaned. She placed her clipboard under her arm and hurried inside to assess the damage.

Harriet gave Max an angry stare. "I'll get you for that," she said.

"It was an accident," replied Max.

"Yeah, right!" snapped Harriet. She glided into the building. Harriet went to the children's section where the rest of the class was waiting.

Max hung back and took in his surroundings. Except for an ancient-looking sardine-faced creature that was dozing over a copy of the *Fin-ancial Times,* there was no one around.

He looked up at the signs tacked to the

various sections of shelving. CORAL SCIENCE,
read the nearest one. He stepped between
two shelves and hurried to the end of the row.
He turned left and passed rows labeled NON-
WATER SPORTS, SCALY HUMOR, AND CARP
PHILOSOPHY. He passed a table with a display
of books. Each book had a picture of a giant
purple gem on the cover and the same title:
Tasmine Crystal.

He hurried on and came to a sign saying
DEEP SEA HISTORY. He dashed down the first
row and ran his finger over the titles. *Crab
Archeology for Beginners*, *A Short History of
Anemones*, *The Court of Lady Shrimpton*.

And then he spotted it: *Where Do We Come
From? A Brief History of Aquatropolis.*

It was a slim volume with a pale blue cover.
He pulled it off the shelf and opened it. Max
scanned the contents page, looking for the
best place to start. The title of chapter three
caught his eye: "A Reflection on our Evolution."

Max turned to the beginning of the chapter and started to read:

It is now accepted by most history experts in Aquatropolis that Humans and Slithers developed side by side.

So that's what these creatures down here

*are called. Slithers!*

As Humans developed from apes, so
Slithers developed from fish. The main
difference between us and Humans is
that in spite of retaining some apelike
features, Humans evolved into a distinct
and totally separate group of beings.

Slithers only evolved up to a point.
We stopped at the stage where we
kept a human half and a fish half.
While Humans were unable to live
underwater, Slithers can live on land
and in water.

*So these guys could come and live with us.
Yikes!*

According to our current ruler, the
Mighty King Flago, it is not fair that . . .

Suddenly, a hand grabbed Max roughly by
the shoulder.

He spun around. It was Mrs. Flint. And she didn't look pleased.

"What under sea do you think you are playing at, young man?" she demanded in a shrill tone. She grabbed him by the ear and led him back to the children's section. "You can't just wander off from the rest of the class like this. And your name isn't even on the class list I was given."

"There must be some mistake," replied Max. He looked around for a possible quick exit.

"Well, none of the other pupils know you. And Harriet started telling me some nonsense about me being your mother." Mrs. Flint narrowed her fishy eyes at him.

Max edged a few steps toward the library's exit. But the teacher caught his elbow. "No way," she said firmly. "You're coming with me. I'm going to find out who you are!"

CHAPTER 8

Max gave Mrs. Flint his most charming smile.
"If you let go of me, I swear I'll tell you who I
am. There's nothing fishy going on. I promise,"
he said. *Apart from you lot!*

Max took Mrs. Flint's arms and pushed her
firmly down onto one of the movable library
stools. Mrs. Flint opened her mouth to protest
while Max put his foot against one of the legs.
He shoved with all his might. The stool sped
off, skimming over the highly polished floor
and taking Mrs. Flint with it. The whole class

burst into laughter. The teacher spun toward the children's section, knocking into books and tables and chairs as she went.

Max didn't wait to see where she ended up. He pushed open the door and sped back into the street. In front of him was a large shopping mall called The Reef Center. He hurried inside. The library had been a good starting point. But he needed more information. Maybe he could find a bookstore.

Then he saw a café that had a huge TV screen in the far corner. The words ARE YOU READY FOR RAY DAY? were plastered across the screen. Seconds later, they were replaced by an image of the earth.

Max stared up at the screen. Would he get some answers? What did Aquatropolis's leader King Flago think wasn't fair about Humans evolving to live on land and Slithers living underwater? And what did this have to do with Ray Day? Max's brain was buzzing as he stepped into the café and walked down the aisle. The tables were bare except for the odd dish of moldy-looking seaweed fritters and seaweed burgers.

Yuck! All they seem to eat in this place is seaweed!

Most of the tables were taken. But there was a spare seat at the one nearest the screen. The other three seats were taken by old Slithers. They had bearded human heads and prawn bodies. One of them was wearing a blue bandana and a large silver earring in his right ear. Their eyes were fixed on the screen.

"Is this seat taken?" Max asked.

The men shook their heads but kept their eyes on screen. Max slid into the chair and turned his attention to the screen.

"RAY DAY will be our day," ran the commentary. "A time for conquering. A time for victory! At last we will get to use our precious Azulin Filter! At last we will . . ."

"To the Azulin Filter!" cried the men at Max's table, raising their glasses.

The Azulin Filter? What on earth is that? And how is it connected to Ray Day?

Max leaned forward and eagerly awaited the next part of the commentary. But the screen suddenly went blank. His heart sank with disappointment. The guys at the table turned to face him.

"So," said the one wearing the blue bandana, "are YOU ready for Ray Day?"

"Er . . . yeah," nodded Max hesitantly. "Totally ready. I'm really looking forward to it!"

"That's the spirit, kid!" the Slither said. "What do you think our chances are against the Humans?"

Max coughed nervously. "Well . . . I think . . . if we fight them, er, properly, we've got a great chance," he replied.

The guys were silent for a few seconds. They suddenly all burst out laughing.

"Good one!"

"Imagine!" another chortled. "Six billion Humans against us! We'd stand a great chance, wouldn't we!"

Other customers who'd heard Max's comment joined in with the laughter.

Max felt his cheeks redden as confusion swept through him. *So Zavonne's wrong. The Slithers aren't going to attack us. They accept*

*they'd be outnumbered. So WHAT is going on?
And how am I going to find out who Ray is?*

Suddenly a series of loud smashes came
from over by the bar. Everyone turned around
to see what was going on. One of the waiters
had been shoved out of the way by a hideous-
looking creature with a vicious shark head.
He'd dropped a large tray of glasses that
crashed to the floor.

The laughter immediately stopped.

"Who's that?" Max whispered.

"Dreydor, captain of the Shark Corps," the
Slither with the bandana whispered.

*The Shark Corps? Now there's a friendly-
sounding organization!*

Max watched as another five of these shark
creatures stormed into the bar. They fanned
out behind Dreydor and showered everyone
with accusing stares.

Dreydor took a few paces forward. He
scanned the terrified faces of the café's

customers. "Many of you know an intruder entered Aquatropolis earlier today. My men and I are doing spot checks all over the city. We believe it might be a whole Human."

Max gulped nervously.

"So anyone wearing a fashion wrap needs to take it off immediately," added Dreydor. "That way we can rule you out."

He paused for a second, and his eyes narrowed. "Unless, of course, one of you is that Human. Then we'll deal with you appropriately."

Max clutched at his wrap. *What do I do?*

He couldn't just hang around waiting for Dreydor and his men to make their way to his table. Max glanced around and scanned his surroundings for an escape route. He wouldn't be able to get to the main entrance undetected, but there was a swing door that led into the kitchen.

"Nothing here, Captain Dreydor!" the Shark

Corps shouted as they continued their search.
They were three tables away from where
Max was sitting when he made his move. He
stood up and hurtled toward the swing door.
Everything on the table went flying.

"STOP HIM!" yelled Dreydor. The captain and
his troops thundered across the room after
Max.

Max reached the door and threw it open.
He dived through and heard it swing back and
catch Dreydor in the face with a bang.

Max fled through the kitchen. He sped past a cart on wheels and a tower of seaweed pizza delivery boxes. He crashed through a door at the end of the kitchen. Max found himself in a deserted hallway at the back of the mall.

It was a service corridor stretching to his right and left. In front of him was a service elevator. He ran over to it and thumped the button. A green light flashed. The elevator was five floors above him. He hit it again, but the display didn't change. *What's wrong with it?*

Behind him he heard shouting. The thudding feet grew nearer. He glanced left and right. He'd never make it to either end of the corridor. He was a fast runner. But these guys had legs three times longer than his. And the elevator was still going nowhere.

"GET HIM!" he heard Dreydor roar.

MISSION 3

CHAPTER 9

Max started to imagine what being eaten
would be like. Then he suddenly had a
brainwave. The Crash Divider! It opened doors
and panels! He pulled it out and slipped
it between the elevator doors. The doors
parted in a second. Max dived through and
immediately felt himself falling.

Max had forgotten that there was no
elevator on the other side of the door! He
looked down for a second. Below him was a
deep pit of darkness.

Max threw his arms out. He desperately searched for something to hold on to. His right hand suddenly found one of the elevator cables. He snatched it and gripped with all his might. Just one slip and he'd be hurtling down the shaft to certain death. Max's heart raced as he reached up with his left hand. He held on as his legs swung beneath him.

He could hear the muffled shouts of the Shark Corps above him. They arrived in the corridor only to find that he'd vanished. Then he picked up the sounds of feet darting in both directions. They must have split up to hunt him down. Max breathed a sigh of relief. He swung around in the pitch-black shaft. The cable he was swinging from suddenly started to move just as he was contemplating how to escape. Max looked up.

The elevator! It was slamming down toward him at breakneck speed. He was about to be seriously squashed!

He could hear the high-pitched screech of the cables as the elevator hurtled toward him. Up and up he flew. Down and down the elevator sped. It was now less than twenty meters above him, smashing down fast.

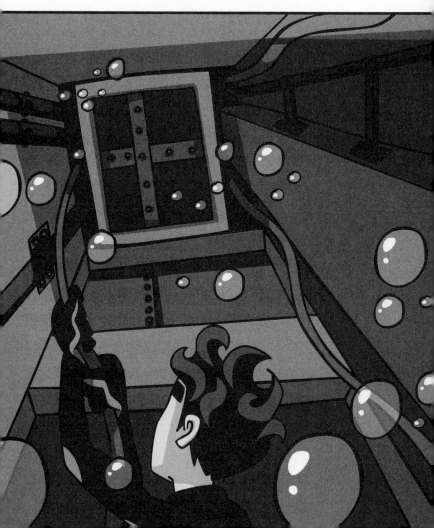

Max winced and let go of the cable. He threw himself against the left-hand wall of the shaft. There was a tiny gap.

He slid himself into the space and felt the rush of the elevator as it crashed past him. But there was nothing to hold onto. A second later Max lost his balance. He toppled back into the shaft. He hurtled down the shaft, screaming in terror, for what seemed like forever. Max landed with a smack on the roof of the elevator. He rolled to his side to break his fall and almost got his head cut off by a metal beam. He shook himself in disbelief as he lay on the roof. The water rushed past him in the darkness.

And then the elevator suddenly started losing speed. It slowed right down. A few seconds later it came to a halt. Max heard people getting out. He waited a few seconds and then twisted a dial on the center of the roof. A circular panel slid open. He dropped

down inside the elevator. A small group of creatures with human heads and carp lower bodies pushed a vending machine into the elevator. They froze in surprise.

"Oh, hi!" Max grinned. He gave them a confident wave. "Problem with some cables. All fixed now."

"Let's just get this thing in," grunted one member of the group.

Max eased past them and out of the elevator as they wedged the machine inside. As the doors closed, he heard a Slither talking. "They're taking younger and younger staff on nowadays, aren't they? He looked like a kid."

Max allowed himself a quick grin before checking the corridors for any sign of the Shark Corps. He let himself out of the building, through a glass door and was back on Main Street. He was trying to make sense of things when he heard a commotion up ahead. A big crowd had gathered. There were excited cheers and whistles. Max hurried to see what was going on.

He saw what all the fuss was about when he reached the crowd. A huge, cylindrical tank with a large opaque panel on the side was being driven down the road. People were pointing at the panel in awe. Max eased his way through the crowd until he got a clear view.

Inside the tank was a huge purple gem. It glittered and twinkled.

"The Tasmine Crystal," he heard someone utter with hushed amazement.

Max instantly remembered the display table in the library. All of those books had been about the Tasmine Crystal. Now here it was. If only he'd stopped at the table and read a bit. Then he might have some idea what the significance of the crystal was. Could it be related in some way to Ray Day? Was it a prize

or war spoil that Ray had won?

"This is so exciting," gushed another Slither. "The Tasmine Crystal and the Azulin Filter together. What a combination!"

So the Tasmine Crystal and the Azulin Filter are connected! But how? And I'm STILL no closer to discovering who Ray is!

The crowd buzzed with excitement. It moved down the road alongside the vehicle. Max was tempted to go with them and check out where the Tasmine Crystal was heading. Then he noticed that a huge trail of bubbles followed behind the tank, forming a trail to where it had come from.

Perhaps I should investigate away from the crowd . . .

The bubbles stretched into the distance. It was worth a try. If he could find where the Crystal came from, he might find out where it was going. And he might get the answers to several other questions too. He looked back down the street and saw Dreydor and his army fly out of the mall. Max checked his wrap. It was securely fastened around his waist. He hurried away.

He didn't stop running until he was well out of sight of the Shark Corps. The twists and twirls of bubbles were still strong. He followed them down several streets until they started thinning out.

Max arrived at the point where the trail had started. It was by an imposing white building with three silver turrets and a huge set of wrought iron gates. SHOAL LABORATORY, read a sign on a high wall to the right of the gates.

A laboratory? I should be able to find out about the Tasmine Crystal here . . .

CHAPTER 10

Just then he heard the loud roar of an engine. He crouched down next to the railing and spotted a large red van approaching the gates.

Max pressed his back against the railing and watched. The van pulled up in front of the gates. A Slither with a salmon head reached out of the driver's window and pressed a switch on a small panel next to the gate.

"Delivery of Carbuncle Sodium Chlorate," the driver spoke into the intercom.

There was a pause. Then the gates made a

clicking sound and started to slowly open. Max seized his chance. He sped over to the back of the van while crouching as low as he could. It was already moving through the gates by the time he reached it.

He scurried underneath and grabbed the exhaust pipe. He pulled himself up, stretching his body along the underside of the van. He hooked his feet on either side. The engine thudded. A flurry of bubbles hit Max in the face. He slammed a hand over his mouth to stop himself from coughing. A few seconds later, the van stopped.

He heard the driver's door open and watched as two jeans-clad human legs touched the ground.

"All present and correct?" he heard a deep voice ask.

"Yeah, this is my last delivery of the day."

"Well, open her up then," ordered the first voice.

Max watched as two sets of feet walked around to the back of the van. He heard a lever being twisted and then a metallic ruffle as the van's shutters were pulled open.

"It's all in there," said the second voice, the driver's.

Both sets of feet left the ground. Max heard boots climbing up onto the van's tailgate. This was followed by a scraping sound as the two creatures stepped into the van to check whatever was inside.

The footsteps clunked above him while he heard muffled voices. A few seconds later, the footsteps went away. The two Slithers jumped down to the ground.

"I'm just going to get the paperwork," said the driver.

Max watched the driver's feet stroll around to the front of the van. *I might find out what's going on if I can hang on here!*

Max congratulated himself on his plan. Then a strong flashlight beam suddenly cut through the darkness under the van. Max shrunk back in horror as the beam almost hit him.

A wave of fear snaked down his spine. He pressed himself against the underside of the van. Max tried to make himself invisible as the flashlight beam swished left, then right. The guard was just making a second, more thorough sweep when the driver called out.

"Can we get the paperwork done? I want a decent lunch break."

The guard paused, sighed, and turned off the flashlight. He got to his feet. Max watched in relief as the Slither walked over to join the driver at the front of the van. Max feared the guard might return with the flashlight, so he quickly crawled along the pipes underneath the van. He reached the end. He stuck his legs out and up onto the tailgate. Pressing down very hard with his toes, he eased the rest of his body out. Then he grabbed the tailgate with his hands. In one swift movement, he flung himself up and onto his feet.

Inside the back of the van was a set of large blue canisters. They were the type used to transport gas. One of them was empty, and the stopper was off. Max moved closer to investigate. He tripped over the stopper and sent it flying.

"What was that?" demanded the guard.

Max heard feet scurrying in his direction. He flung himself forward. He contorted his body and just managed to get into the canister and slam the stopper on as the guard's feet hit the tailgate again. The footsteps thudded in Max's direction. He heard the guard unscrew the stopper on another canister. And then the footsteps headed straight for his canister.

OK. The game's up. Hand me over for Dreydor's supper.

Another agonizing thirty seconds passed. Then he felt himself being turned onto his back as his canister was lowered down onto the tailgate. It was rolled off the back of the van and along the ground for what seemed like forever. Max's body spun over and over inside the canister. He felt the canister being pushed over the lip of a doorjam.

Finally, he came to a halt. He heard the footsteps retreating.

He waited. One minute. Two minutes. Silence. Should he go and investigate? Or stay put?

Max took a deep breath. He pushed the stopper out and poked his head a fraction over the rim.

He blinked in the bright glare of spotlights. As his eyes adjusted to the light, he saw that he was in a huge, white-walled laboratory. Three Slithers in white lab coats sat at workstations at the far side of the room. They wore surgical gloves and punched red and yellow flashing buttons on large metallic panels fixed in front of them.

There was no one on Max's side of the lab. There was just a row of shining laptops.

Max kept his eyes firmly on the lab-coat crew while he pushed himself through the opening of the canister. He lowered himself silently to the floor.

He stayed low to the ground as he crawled over to the row of laptops. He raised his right hand, reached up for the mouse, and clicked. The screen saver disappeared. The words ENTER PASSWORD appeared.

I'll just have to guess. I need to get some information on these guys!

He slid his fingers onto the keyboard and typed in RAY DAY.

INCORRECT PASSWORD flashed across the screen.

He tried AQUATROPOLIS.

INCORRECT PASSWORD the screen replied.

Next he tried TASMINE CRYSTAL.

INCORRECT PASSWORD.

Max scratched his head in frustration.

He could be here for days and not be able

to log on. It could be any word or number
or combination of both. He thought about
everything he'd seen and heard since he'd
been in Aquatropolis.

*The Slithers seem to be massively in awe of
their king. Why not give that a go?*

He typed in KING FLAGO.

INCORRECT PASSWORD the monitor bleeped
back.

Max bit his bottom lip thoughtfully.

He added the words THE MIGHTY to KING
FLAGO.

The screen went blank for a few seconds.
Max feared it had switched itself off after his
multiple incorrect passwords. But then the
words CORRECT PASSWORD ACCESS GRANTED
flashed back at Max.

Yes!

He almost shouted with relief but realized
that probably wasn't a good strategy for
remaining undetected. About twenty flashing

red folders appeared on the screen. He checked that the Slithers hadn't noticed him and began to scan the folders quickly.

WAVE TECH.

DAILY NOTES.

LAB FINANCE.

TASMINE CRYSTAL.

Max's eyes widened. He double-clicked the TASMINE CRYSTAL folder. It opened immediately and showed a large collection of individual documents. There was one that grabbed Max's attention.

It was called TAS CRYST + AQ FILT – AQUATROPOLIS CENTRAL HALL – PUBLIC PRESENTATION. Max opened the file.

The opening paragraphs were thanking various members of something called the Ray Day Public Committee.

This looks boring and useless . . .

But things started to get more interesting in paragraph five. By paragraph six, he was hooked.

Our engineers had completed the highly complex Tasmine Crystal on time. All that we needed to do now was to create the Azulin Filter. You're all aware that the conditions for creating the Filter happen once every ten thousand years.

Ten thousand years?

We were ready for the exact window of time when deep-sea conditions were absolutely perfect. The process was successful. The Azulin Filter is now complete. Early trials have been a glowing success. Linking the Filter's huge powers to the Crystal's antigravitational pull has produced spectacular results, even when only a tiny fraction of possible power is activated.

Antigravitational pull?

We therefore conclude that all is ready for Ray Day. Success is assured. Our future will be bountiful and plentiful.

Bountiful and plentiful . . . what?!
Max stared at the screen and racked his brain. If gravitational pull kept things down, then antigravitational pull must keep things up. But what things were being kept up? And for what purpose? And how did this Azulin Filter link to the Crystal's pull?
Max's brain hurt with trying to work it out. *This is getting seriously scientific!*

Then a thought suddenly struck him.
He remembered the "freak flood" that had
temporarily engulfed Decca Island.

Could it be that the antigravitational pull of
the Tasmine Crystal pulled up water?

The report said that early trials had been a
glowing success. What if the flooding of the
island was an "early trial" for something much
bigger? Maybe linking the Azulin Filter and the
Tasmine Crystal would pull up a far greater
amount of water. What if the amount was so
large it could do permanent damage?

He scrolled down to the next paragraph but
was interrupted by a metallic clunking sound.
He looked up. The Slithers in lab coats were
gone. Giant steel shutters were closing over
every exit.

Max leaped up and started running. His feet
pounded along the shiny lab floor. The shutters
were almost completely down. Max ran faster.
He dove forward onto his knees. He turned

himself into a human thunderbolt. The smooth
floor was a perfect launch pad. His whole
body flew forward at incredible speed. His
way out would be blocked in three seconds.
He leaned back as far as he could and closed
his eyes while hurtling forward. The top of his
head missed the underside of a shutter by a
millimeter. But he was through!

MISSION 3

CHAPTER 11

Max crashed against a wall and ricocheted off.
He came to a halt in the middle of a narrow
corridor. The sound of shutters closing echoed
throughout the whole building. Max turned
right and sped across the floor. Twenty meters
down he spotted a small skylight window
in the ceiling. He pulled himself up onto a
window ledge. Max stretched as far as he could
and caught hold of the window catch. He
twisted it, pushed the window open, and dived
through.

He found himself on a flat roof near the front of the building. The high gates up ahead were still open a fraction. The gap was just wide enough for him to squeeze through. Max checked to make sure there was no one around. He sprinted to the edge of the roof and leaped down toward the gates. But just as he reached them, a huge line of Shark Corps heavies emerged from every doorway.

Max pulled the Bubble Exploder out of his pocket before any of them could take a step. He twisted off the cap, snatched out the bubble ring, and blew.

Bubbles shot out from the ring and straight toward the Shark Corps.

They had no time to react.

The bubbles zipped forward, creating a dense, swirling mass of power that flew toward them. The force hit the Shark Corps and flung them backward. They yelled and crashed into one another.

Max looked at the bubble ring admiringly. *Cool!* He yanked the gates open and fled. He retraced his steps back to Main Street.

I have to get back to the Tasmine Crystal. It looks like the Slithers want to use it to create a giant flood to wash us away!

Max sped to the end of the street. He turned the corner. The road ahead was empty. He sprinted down it. His feet pounded on the ground. Up ahead was another corner. He skidded around it and froze.

There in front of him were three members of the Shark Corps blocking his path. Max quickly spun around. To his horror, three more of them stood in the road behind him. Others appeared from a doorway on his left. And another team of the vicious fish force emerged from the right. He was ambushed!

And last but not least, the hulking figure of Captain Dreydor appeared. He was on top of a tall building just up ahead. Dreydor stepped

off the building's roof and floated down to the ground.

"Thought you were being clever with that elevator stunt earlier, didn't you?" he snarled.

"It wasn't bad, was it?" laughed Max, trying to buy some time.

"Well, the time for fun and games is over," hissed Dreydor.

Max swallowed nervously. What he needed was a gadget, and quickly! He reached into his pocket for the Power Shoot. The space where he'd put it was empty! He desperately rooted around for it. But it had totally disappeared.

Dreydor saw Max's terror and roared with laughter.

"Come on, boys!" he declared. "It's feeding time!"

Dreydor and his men started to move in on Max. Their cruel eyes locked onto him.

MAX FLASH

OK. Time's up. It's over. Finished. Kaput. The end of the road. Will Dreydor feed on me and throw the leftover scraps to the others? Or will it be a communal feast? And what part of me will they eat first?

These questions zipped through his mind as Dreydor and his hideous Shark Corps closed in. All around Max were huge jaws full of gleaming, fiercely sharp teeth, ready to do some serious damage. He didn't stand a chance.

CHAPTER 12

Max closed his eyes. Every muscle in his body clenched with dread.

"STOP!" a powerful voice thundered.

Max opened one eye. His head was halfway inside Dreydor's mouth.

Dreydor froze. Max could feel the captain's teeth skimming the top of his hair.

The members of the Shark Corps bowed their heads low. "Behold the Mighty King Flago!" they chorused.

Dreydor pulled his jaw back. Max breathed

a sigh of relief and looked around for the Mighty King Flago. There was no sign of him anywhere.

And then Max's gaze fell on the ground. He spotted a tiny crab with very short human legs and a gold crown resting on his head.

Surely this little critter isn't the all-powerful king!

For a creature so small, King Flago had an impressively loud voice. "I apologize for the actions of my police force, young man." King Flago advanced to Max's side and looked up at him. "They do a marvelous job down here. But they can get . . . how shall I put this . . . a bit over excited. This Human boy means no harm," he declared. He gazed around at the Shark Corps. They all still had their heads bowed.

"Our loyalties are to you, oh mighty King," whispered Captain Dreydor.

"Our loyalties are to you, oh mighty King," chorused the others.

"Excellent," smiled King Flago. "But you can leave him in my care now."

Dreydor lifted his head. "Whatever you command," he stated.

'Yes," chimed the others. "Whatever you com—"

"STOP REPEATING EVERYTHING I SAY!" roared Dreydor.

"Sorry, boss," a few of them muttered.

King Flago rolled his eyes. "You will accompany me to my palace," he said to Max.

Max took a deep breath. He was sure that time was running out. But faced with a choice between the king and the Shark Corps, he'd take the king any day.

"Of course, King Flago," Max nodded. He grinned at Dreydor. "Nice to have met you."

Dreydor snarled but said nothing.

King Flago strode off toward the end of the street. He had to go very slowly because of his

size. He headed around the corner to where a tiny black stretch limo was parked.

"I would invite you in for a ride," said the king, "but I think there would be a passenger size issue. However, my palace is big enough to house even the largest of beings. It isn't far."

A door slid open. Flago disappeared inside the limo. Its engine sprang to life, and it pulled away. Max walked behind. He looked over his shoulder. Dreydor and his band of thugs were staring furiously at him.

The limo turned a corner and pulled up in front of a massive gold palace. The limo door opened and the king emerged. Flago walked briskly across a gravel concourse. Max followed at the king's side and took a quick peek behind him. There was no sign of the Shark Corps. For the moment, at least.

"We'll go straight to the banquet room," said the king.

I need to get back to the Crystal. But a few

minutes in here should be OK. And maybe
Flago will fill me in on Ray Day.

Max and the king marched inside the
building and across a huge red-carpeted lobby.
They went down a long corridor, up a set of
sweeping stairs, and through a set of double
doors.

Max stopped for a second on entering the
Royal Banquet Suite. It was majorly impressive.
The Suite was as good as any of the pictures
he'd seen of rooms in Buckingham Palace. A
huge table was set with gleaming silver cutlery
and covered with a white linen tablecloth.

"I hope this will be comfortable enough for
you," declared the king.

"Yeah . . . great," agreed Max.

King Flago seated himself on a minuscule
marble throne. Max sat down on a normal-
sized gold dining chair. A large group of
servant Slithers with human heads and trout
bottom halves swept into the room. They

carried an array of covered silver dishes. The servants bowed low to Flago as they deposited the trays on the table.

Wow, what a feast! There must be fifty dishes here!

Max's eyes bulged. And his stomach rumbled. A quick bite to eat to give him energy for the rest of his mission would be a good idea . . .

King Flago nodded at the servants. They glided out of the room as silently and smoothly as they had entered.

"Please," said the king with a nod, "try as many as you like."

Max pulled off the lid of the silver tray nearest him. It revealed a small plate of seaweed fritters.

OK, OK. Not a great first choice. I'll be luckier with my second choice.

Max pried off a second lid and discovered . . . seaweed cakes. The third revealed . . . seaweed

kebabs. He pulled off lid after lid. Max's
expectations faded away, as did his appetite.
Every single dish offered a different type
of seaweed.

"Disappointing, isn't it?" remarked King

Flago. He fixed two very beady eyes on Max. "Unfortunately, that's all we have left down here," he explained. "The years of plenty are long gone."

"Your diet does seem a bit . . . limited," agreed Max.

"And it's not only the food," sighed the king. "It's all of our resources. We've run dry. Oh, the irony!"

Suddenly Max understood. *This must be the Slithers' motivation for an assault on the earth above. They have no resources left, so they need to steal more. And the only way they can think of doing this is to flood the place using the Tasmine Crystal and the Azulin Filter. They want to drown humankind. Then they can step in and bag up the necessary resources! Bingo!*

"Anyway," said the king, "tell me all about you. How did you get down here? How did you find out about us? I'm fascinated."

Max shuffled uncomfortably in his seat and eyed the room's only exit. *I need to make a move, and soon.*

"I've always loved diving," he lied. "This time I thought I'd go much deeper than usual."

"But you knew we existed?"

"No," answered Max. He shook his head and glanced at the exit again. "I just . . . chanced on it. You know, a lucky break."

"And who sent you?" inquired King Flago with a smiling nod of encouragement.

"No one," lied Max again. "I mean, no one official. I was on a diving trip with my family."

The king looked puzzled. "But you have no diving gear!"

"It's been lovely talking to you," said Max. He stood up quickly.

Metal clamps sprang out from under Max's chair and wrapped themselves around his wrists and ankles. The chair tilted backward.

Max found himself lying flat on his back, his wrists and ankles tightly bound.

CHAPTER 13

"I gave you a chance to speak the truth, Human boy," yelled King Flago. He hopped onto Max's chest and pointed a claw at him. "But you told me lies!"

Max flicked his wrists. The clamps held tight. "I'm telling you the truth," he protested.

"No you are NOT!" shrieked King Flago. "I realized that trouble was afoot as soon as I heard there was an earth intruder down here. The coincidence is too great to believe!"

"Coincidence?" asked Max.

"Don't play the innocent with me!" snapped the king. "Ray Day has arrived. And you just happen to chance upon us? I've never heard anything so ridiculous! The waters will be rising shortly. Our great mission will be under way!"

The waters will be rising shortly! I was right! The Slithers are going to flood Earth!

"Hang on a minute," cut in Max. "Ray Day is today?"

"Don't pretend you didn't know," snarled the king. "You've seen the crowds. You've seen the Tasmine Crystal. You've even managed to get inside our laboratory!"

"OK. OK, I didn't chance on your city," said Max. "I was sent here to explore. But I swear I didn't know anything about Ray and his famous Day."

The king leaned forward. "You are not a very convincing liar!" he declared. "Making out that you think Ray is a creature! You think you're

being clever don't you? Think you can fool the
Mighty King Flago!"

Max's brain had gone into overdrive. *Ray
isn't a creature? What have I missed? If it
doesn't refer to a creature, what is it?*

"Hang on a second," said Max. He tried to
make sense of all of these new facts. "If you
hate me so much, why didn't you just let the
Shark Corps eat me?"

"And say goodbye to potentially crucial
information?" sneered the king. "Not a chance!
We're all ready down here. But you may have
vital news about what's happening above the
surface. You know whether or not our Human
'friends' are expecting our calling card."

"I told you," said Max firmly. "Neither I nor
any other humans are expecting anything. We
didn't even know you existed."

Max twisted his wrists and ankles under the
metal clamps.

"Is that why you sent that ship and those

divers here recently?" demanded the king.

Max recalled the DFEA diving team who'd been attacked.

"We spotted them crawling all over the island," said the king darkly. "When they dived in, we had to stop them. It was too risky. They might have found us and spoiled everything. So we sent them packing. We hoped we'd heard the last of any reckless Human explorers. And then you show up."

Why are the Slithers so concerned about the DFEA finding something on Decca Island? Think, Max, think!

"Look," said Max, "I honestly don't know what you're talking about. So just let me go. I won't trouble you again and then—"

"Let you go?" roared the king with an evil glint in his eyes. "Oh no, no, no, no! I will get information out of you. If it's the last thing you do."

Max looked up at the weedy little crab man.

Flago could pinch him a bit. But that would hardly hurt. It certainly wouldn't make him spill any beans on the DFEA and his mission.

Max felt reassured by this. Then Flago looked to the door and shouted, "Poison 8. I want you in here, NOW!"

Max gulped nervously. *Poison 8? That doesn't sound like the name of a sweet and gentle creature who is going to tickle the information out of me.*

Seconds later he heard a squelching sound. A giant monster slunk into the room. Its top half was squidlike, with eight long, blue tentacles. Each tentacle ended in a glowing orange tip. Its bottom half was human and wearing combat trousers and army boots.

"Allow me to introduce Poison 8," grinned

King Flago. "See the orange points at the ends of his tentacles? These sacs are filled with some of the most powerful poison ever. Just one touch will send tremors of agony through your body. But it won't kill you. My beautiful pet can inflict endless pain on his victims. As you can imagine, he is very skilled at loosening people's tongues."

Poison 8 glared at Max. He let out a large burp. "I'm ready, Your Majesty," he announced. "Just give me the word."

"Soon I will let you loose on him," cried the king. "But first, a few words of instruction."

The king beckoned to Poison 8. The two of them walked to the far side of the room and started whispering. Max got straight to work. His all-time hero was Harry Houdini. Houdini was the world's greatest escapologist. He had specialized in handcuff escapes. Max had studied his methods in great detail. Max had pushed his hands and feet toward

the clamps when they had snapped down on him. That way, the clamps had secured themselves on his forearms and shins instead. Max kept one eye on the huddled conversation in the corner. He pulled his wrists and ankles toward him. He silently wriggled out of the clamps.

He stared at Poison 8's tentacles. Neutralizing their poisonous threat would be tricky. Flago turned and stared at Max. "I suggest you talk quickly," he snapped. "That way you will avoid a marathon of pain!"

And with that, the tiny crab king bustled out of the room. Max gulped. Poison 8 would see that Max was free from the clamps if he took even the quickest look.

I have to keep his eyes on mine.

"Poison 8," said Max. He stared deep into the squid man's eyes. "Perhaps we could come to some sort of arrangement?"

Poison 8 belched. "I shouldn't have had

those seaweed burgers," he muttered.

"Poison 8, your tentacles really are impressive."

"Don't try to flatter me," replied Poison 8. He moved closer. He did seem to like the compliment, though. "The Mighty King Flago has told me what he needs from you. I will follow his commands."

"Sure," smiled Max. "I understand. But there is something you ought to know about the Mighty King Flago. He told me a couple of mean things about you."

"I don't believe you," replied the giant squid. But he was beginning to look confused.

It was the break Max needed. He leaped off the chair. With incredible speed, he grabbed one of Poison 8's tentacles just above the orange tip. In a maze of swirling arm movements, he tied the tentacle up with the seven others. Max stood back to admire his handiwork.

Poison 8 tried to scream. But all that came out was a tiny whimper.

"Hopefully I won't be seeing you around," said Max. He hurried across the room to the door. "But if I see the king, I'll send him your kindest regards."

CHAPTER 15

Max sped out into the corridor. He saw
a servant up ahead. She turned left and
disappeared through a doorway. Max set off
and was thankful that he'd memorized the
way he'd come in. He made it back to the
stairs leading down to the lobby without
seeing anyone. Two servants were standing
in the lobby entrance. They were deep in
conversation.

Max looked around. He spotted a large vase
of pink flowers. He grabbed it and threw it over

the railing to the far side of the lobby. Max ducked out of sight. The vase crashed onto the red carpet, sending shards of glass and pink flowers everywhere. The servants spun around. They saw no one and hurried over to clean up the mess. Max ran down the stairs. He scurried across the lobby and out of the palace.

The street outside was chaotic. There were alarms sounding. Slithers were running in every direction. A huge searchlight beamed out over the whole of Aquatropolis to hunt him down. *So much for being undercover!*

As Max watched the light, he suddenly realized something.

That's it! Ray Day must refer to a ray of LIGHT. That's why the Slithers were worried about humans snooping around Decca Island. Because of its lighthouse! They must have used it in the initial flooding experiment. That means the Tasmine Crystal and Azulin Filter must be on their way there now. I must hurry!

His thoughts were just going into overdrive. Then he heard a deafening roar.

"SEIZE HIM!"

Max spun around. He was horrified to see the Shark Corps and Dreydor a short way down the street. And this time they had wheels. Each of them was on a huge silver motorbike. They were gunning straight for him. Dreydor was at the head of the pack.

Dreydor's bike was almost upon him when Max dived to the side. The bike swerved violently and threw Dreydor into the middle of the road. He thudded to the ground. Dreydor's bike crashed onto the road beside him.

Max didn't waste a second. He ran over and picked up the bike. Max leaped onto it. He twisted the throttle to activate the jet propulsion. The bike lunged forward. Max performed an unplanned but spectacular wheelie. He looked up to see a row of sharks. They revved their engines and snarled in fury.

The chase was on!

Max urged the bike forward. He made a beeline for the surface. Beneath the roar of the bike's engine he could hear the spluttering roars of the engines behind him. Max took a quick look over his shoulder. He had about twenty meters on them.

He had to make it to the surface and stop their Tasmine Crystal plan, whatever it was. Up and up through the water he sped. Max was relieved to see that he was keeping his lead. He kept on giving the bike

nudges and making turns to try to shove the Shark Corps off his tail. They were rock steady in their pursuit. They meant business.

Max rode higher, and sights of fish and plant life rushed past him. He sped past a giant yellow-and-red coral and a school of silver fish.

I must be getting near to the surface.

But there was still no sign of the waterline. Then Max heard an engine roar unlike the others. This one sounded like a massive speedboat. Max looked back. His heart leaped with fear. It was Dreydor! This time he was riding an enormous orange-and-silver quad bike. It was much more powerful and speedy than the Shark Corps's bikes. And Dreydor was catching up to Max.

Max hit the throttle again. His bike lunged forward, but it made no difference. Dreydor was still closing the gap. By the look on his face, he hadn't quite forgiven Max for not becoming a tasty snack.

Max weaved left and right. He darted here and there, trying to shake off Dreydor. But he was no match for the captain's high-speed bike. He felt a sickening thud as the front of Dreydor's bike nudged the back of his . . .

NO!

Max's bike spun and nearly threw him off. As he righted himself, Dreydor drew up beside him. There was a huge grin plastered across his face. Max panicked and kicked out. His leg smashed against the side of the captain's bike. But it had as much effect as a butterfly wing. Dreydor howled with laughter, showing his terrifying set of teeth.

Come on, come on. Think of a plan or you'll be fish food!

Max suddenly spotted a large rock formation up ahead. He gunned the throttle and rode straight toward it. At the last minute, he turned his bike to the right. He missed the rocks by millimeters. The rocks took Dreydor

by surprise. But instead of smashing into them, he veered to the other side.

Max emerged at the far end of the rocks. Dreydor appeared on the other side. Dreydor grinned with the scent of victory. Max racked his brains. *What would Houdini do in a situation like this?* It was a stupid question. Houdini had never been on an underwater motorbike being chased by a gruesome half-shark, half-human madman.

Max began to despair. Then he looked up and spotted it. The surface! It was still some way off. But he was getting close. Max was full of excitement and relief. He took his eye off Dreydor for a couple of seconds. This left him open to attack. Dreydor reached out and grabbed Max's right shoulder. Max pulled to the left. His bike skimmed off in the other direction. Max broke away from Dreydor's grasp. But as he did so he heard a strange ripping sound.

He looked down at his shoulder. To his horror, he saw a large tear in his Second Skin Suit. Max had just started to assess the full extent of the damage when water suddenly gushed into his nose.

MAX FLASH MISSION 3

Disaster! The rip had broken the breathing mechanism of the Suit. He had no oxygen! Immediately he closed his mouth and nose. He swallowed a fair amount of water in the process. In the madness of the moment, Dreydor struck again. He leaped off his bike and grabbed Max by the throat. A thin smile appeared on his face.

Max realized instantly what the captain was doing. *He's going to keep me down here until I drown!*

Max glanced back and saw the other bikes approaching. Dreydor's army had arrived.

Zavonne had said that Max's ability to hold his breath underwater could come in handy. But he could only manage three minutes.

Any more than that and I'll be history!

There was no way he was going without a fight. Max gritted his teeth and gave Dreydor a hard punch on the nose.

Dreydor let out a yelp of pain and let go of Max. Max somersaulted through the water and landed on Dreydor's floating bike. He cranked the throttle, and the bike flew forward. Max grabbed the handlebars. He directed the bike straight up for the surface. He knew he had very little time to get there. His breath was holding. But he was beginning to feel pressure in his lungs.

Dreydor and the Shark Corps charged after him.

I can't hold my breath for much longer!

Max could feel himself getting weaker. But the shimmering surface was close. And with one last mighty push, the bike shot forward and crashed out of the water.

It flew up into the air, taking Max with it. Max let go of the handlebars and tumbled through the air. He landed with a crash back in the water. He plunged back down and saw Dreydor and his heavies heading straight for him.

Max turned and swam back up to the surface. He kicked frantically. He broke through and saw the dark, black sky. Silver stars sparkled overhead. About a hundred meters away was Decca Island. Max swam ahead in a furious front crawl, trying desperately to reach dry land. He heard gigantic splashes behind him as the other bikes sped out of the water. Their riders were suspended in midair for a second before crashing back into the ocean.

Max swam on. He reached the sloping bank of jagged rocks in front of the island. He scrambled out of the water. He grabbed at the rocks and dragged himself clear. He took a quick peek back. The Shark Corps were powering their way toward him.

Max took off across the rocks. Stretching up above him was the lighthouse and its rotating beam of light. Max stared up. He lost his footing and slipped. He gashed his knee, but he steadied himself and pushed on.

On and up Max climbed. He neared the top of the rocks and spotted something that made his heart leap with fear. On the other side of the lighthouse, the Tasmine Crystal was placed on top of a steel pole. Suspended a hundred meters in the air, it was held in place by a troop of sharks stationed in the water below. The crystal's sides glittered in the moonlight. It looked like a giant orb of purple fire.

Max saw that it was the exact same height as the light rotating in the lighthouse. But the light shining out from the lighthouse wasn't an ordinary beam. It was a deep shade of bright violet.

The Slithers must have already attached the Azulin Filter to the light for Ray Day! I've got to hurry. The completion of my mission is so very close!

Max upped his pace. He ran as fast as he
could. He clambered over the rocks and toward
the lighthouse door. He looked up and saw
that the light had begun to slow down.

*When the Azulin Filter shines the light
onto the Crystal, it must activate the
antigravitational pull. I have to knock the
beam off course!*

Max grabbed the door handle and gave it
a twist. It was firmly locked. He barged his
shoulder against it. There was absolutely no

movement. He looked upward again. The lighthouse light was now almost stationary.

"STAY AWAY FROM THE LIGHT!" screamed Dreydor as he scrambled over the rocks behind him.

But Max was in no mood to obey any command from the freakish shark-head. He hurried around the side of the lighthouse. He spotted a long black metallic ladder rising to the top. Max sprang onto the first rung and began to climb. The light above him was grinding to a complete halt. Its eerie violet glow prepared to hit the Tasmine Crystal.

Max sped up the ladder. But he was running out of time. The special filtered light from the lighthouse stopped. Its immense ray of violet light hit the Tasmine Crystal full-on. The Crystal's surfaces lit up. Sparks of light shot down toward the water.

No!

Max grabbed the next rung and hurried on.

The waters below the Crystal were starting to froth and make a fearsome sound. The water began to rise into the air.

The antigravitational pull! It's started!

And this wasn't just a few little drops of water. This was the most enormous surge. A massive, ever-increasing vortex of water was streaming upward. And it kept on coming.

"YOU WILL NOT STOP RAY DAY!" screamed Dreydor.

Max looked down. Dreydor was climbing up the ladder behind him. There were five other Shark Corps guys farther down. Max heard a click as a bolt just below him broke away from the lighthouse wall. There was another click. Two bolts above him came away and fell to the ground. There was far too much weight on the ladder.

It's going to come unstuck and take us all with it!

There was a series of clicks and pops. Nuts

and bolts rained down. Max looked out to sea.
The massive tide of water was still rising in the
air. It grew bigger and bigger. The land would
be completely submerged when it crashed
back down! The ladder was now swaying
dangerously from side to side as it was ripped
further and further off the wall.

Max pushed on. He was now only a few
meters from the light. He pulled himself onto a
slim ledge when he reached the top. The floor
was very slippery and coated in grease. Max
crawled toward the circular drum of metal that
held the light.

I have to stop the Ray's focus on the Crystal!

The mass of water was rising fast. It was
already hundreds of meters high. Max took
hold of the metal drum and tried to twist it.
There was absolutely no give. It was firmly
rooted to the spot. He tried again, but it didn't
budge.

"I COMMAND YOU TO HALT!"

Max looked around. Dreydor was half-sliding, half-crawling toward him.

Max again tried to move the drum. It was no good.

I have to shift the Ray, I HAVE TO!

"Give up," hissed Dreydor. "You've tried and failed. Come away from the light. I won't hurt you. Trust me."

Max gave a short and bitter laugh. "I trust you less than your weedy, lying king," he snapped.

"How dare you insult the Mighty King Flago!" roared the captain.

But Max had no time for an argument. He'd just spotted something. On the surface of the drum was a tiny oval opening just big enough for him to squeeze through.

He grinned as he contorted himself. He slipped inside the drum. He relished Dreydor's howl of horror. Max knew he was running out of time to set the light off-course before the

tower of water grew too powerful. He threw
his whole weight against the side of the drum.
There was no movement.

*Come on! Earth will have the biggest bath
in history if you don't do something!*

Max gritted his teeth. He summoned every
single ounce of energy he possessed. He
slammed his whole body against the side of
the drum. There was a slight creaking noise as
the drum cranked the tiniest fraction to the
left.

Do it again!

Max threw himself at the wall again.

This time the drum groaned and shifted
several centimeters. The beam of light moved a
fraction more.

The light wasn't completely shining on the
Tasmine Crystal anymore. Its antigravitational
pull was broken. The gigantic sheets of swirling
water stopped in midair and began to retrace
their steps.

"NOOOO!" bellowed Dreydor from outside the drum.

But it was too late. The water that had been heading so forcefully upward was now smashing back down. And it was going to pulverize the lighthouse.

Max had to move fast!

CHAPTER 18

Where was the Power Shoot? Max reached into
the pocket of his Second Skin Suit and rooted
around. To his joy, he felt the green-and-black
marble in the lining.

*The DFEA really needs to employ some
better tailors!* He pressed the tiny red button
on its surface. The water hurtled down toward
the top of the lighthouse. Max shot a hundred
meters up into the air. He hovered there. He
could see Dreydor and all of the Shark Corps
being thrown over the rocks and tossed back

into the sea.

The water hit the Tasmine Crystal. It shattered into thousands of fragments that rained down into the sea. The steel pole that had been holding the Crystal sunk. So did the Shark Corps troopers who had been holding it up.

Max remained perched in the air as the water continued to rain down. But as he watched the flow of water subside, the effects of the Power Shoot wore off. He dropped down into the ocean below.

He hit the water and sunk downward. He kicked back up to the surface with some powerful leg strokes. Max had to tread water as he reached for the blue cord on his Second

Skin Suit. Snub would be here in ten minutes.

Max kept on checking the waterline for signs of the Shark Corps. But the waters were clear. He saw no menacing shapes about to break out. He slowly began to relax a bit, even though he was neck-deep in cold water.

I did it! The lab computer had said the conditions for creating the Azulin Filter occurred once every ten thousand years. The Slithers would have to wait a long time to try to pull a stunt like this again.

Max floated calmly, listening for the sound of Snub's approaching boat. Without warning, something clasped his feet. Max was being dragged downward. His head dipped under the water. He held his breath. He looked down to see what was holding onto his feet. It was Dreydor, with a more crazed look than ever.

"Thought you'd get away with destroying Ray Day, did you?" snarled the captain. His eyes burned with hate.

Max was about to reply. Then he remembered he'd get a huge lungful of water if he spoke. So he just shook his head.

"Say goodbye to the world, Human boy!" cackled Dreydor.

Max anticipated the snarling Slither's next move. Dreydor lunged up and opened his huge jaws. He was prepared to bite Max's head off. But Max was ready. Max reached out and grabbed something floating beside him in the water. Dreydor's teeth flew toward him. It was a chunk of the Tasmine Crystal. He stuffed it into the captain's mouth just as his jaws snapped shut. Dreydor howled in agony.

Max took advantage of Dreydor's pain. He aimed a powerful kung fu kick at his stomach. The captain howled again and shot downward into the murky depths. Max gave him a quick good-bye wave. He kicked up to the surface. He felt a strong grip pulling him up.

Not another Shark Corps heavy!

But the grip belonged to Snub, who yanked him out of the water and over the side of the boat. Max fell onto the boat's floor.

"Let's get out of here!" Max croaked.

Snub didn't need telling twice. He pulled at the engine cord. The boat shot off into the night. Max heard Dreydor's frenzied whine of defeat as the boat sped away from the island.

"What was that?" asked Snub while looking at Max with amazement.

Max took a deep breath and sat up. "OK," he began. "Right at the bottom of the sea, there's this amazing city called Aquatropolis . . ."

MAX FLASH MISSION 3

CHAPTER 19

Zavonne stared out frostily at Max from the plasma screen in the room below the Flash family's cellar. She had spent the last hour debriefing him in detail about his experiences in the depths of the ocean.

"And you're sure about the Slithers not being able to repeat this plan?" asked Zavonne.

"They could build another Tasmine Crystal. But it won't be any use if they don't have this. In fact, they'd have to wait ten thousand years to make another one!"

Max reached into his pocket and pulled out the Azulin Filter. He'd snatched it just before the water had hit the lighthouse.

Zavonne gazed at it in silence.

OK. Maybe, just maybe, I'm going to get some praise!

A metal drawer on the wall began to flash.

"Open it and place the Azulin Filter inside," Zavonne said.

Max walked over. He opened the drawer and gently placed the Filter inside.

"Now close it," demanded Zavonne.

Max followed her instruction.

Zavonne was silent for a few seconds. "Your parents must be pleased at your safe return."

Max nodded. His mom and dad had hugged the life out of him. Then they told him they wanted to hear every single detail about the mission after his debrief with Zavonne.

"There is, however, an issue of great concern to me," noted Zavonne curtly.

Come on, Zavonne! I've just stopped the Earth from being totally washed out. Don't tell me off for anything!

"It's the Second Skin Suit," said Zavonne. "I did tell you to bring it back in one piece."

Is she for real?

"Yes," replied Max defensively. "But you didn't know I'd be facing Captain Dreydor and the Shark Corps."

"True," mused Zavonne. "But repairing the Suit will be very costly and time-consuming."

"It was ripped in the course of action," Max pointed out. "There was nothing I could do."

Zavonne considered this for a few seconds. "I won't belabor the point," she declared. "I just want to remind you to be extra careful when using DFEA materials."

"Yes, Zavonne," answered Max.

"Right then," she said in a brisk, businesslike fashion. "Our paths may cross again soon."

Max didn't get a chance to reply. The image of Zavonne disappeared. And the screen went blank.

At dinner, Max kept his promise. He went into every detail of his mission. His dad got up after the meal to start cleaning up.

"We dealt with Mutant Sandmen," said his mom with a smile. "But the Shark Corps sounds a lot more fierce."

"They are," replied Max. "And they're still down there."

"Well, at least they won't be trying to flood the Earth again," said his dad.

"Yes," agreed his mom. "Keeping the Azulin Filter was brilliant. We're really proud of you."

At least someone appreciates me!

His dad flung a kitchen towel in his
direction. Max caught it and looked at him in
shock.

"You're not serious, Dad?"

"What?" his dad laughed. "Let you off
drying the dishes because you've defeated the
Slithers? No chance!"

Max grimaced and picked up the first plate.

*I've just managed to save the world from a
watery grave, and my reward is drying duty?
How outrageous is that?*

EPILOGUE

Down in Aquatropolis, the Mighty King Flago had just given Captain Dreydor the most immense ear-bashing of all time. He sat alone in the palace banquet room. The doors opened. A line of servants entered. They carried a selection of silver trays. The servants came to a stop and placed the trays down on the table. The king didn't move.

The headwaiter gave a nod. The servants pulled off the tray lids in one swift movement. King Flago let out a shriek and banged his claws on the table.

"I HATE SEAWEED!" he yelled.

MAX
FLASH
MISSION 4
GRAVE DANGER

Jonny Zucker